One chilly morning, Kitty pounced onto Farmer's fresh pile of laundry.

It was a perfect fit.

Kitty sauntered outside for a
trip around the barnyard.

"Kitty," said Dog, "what are you doing in those underpants?"

Kitty looked as proud as a kitty could.
"It's a coat," said Kitty.

And there was. Barely.

Kitty and Dog strutted by the barn.

"It's a COAT," said Kitty and Dog with such conviction that Pig readily agreed.

"Well, I've always wanted a coat," said Pig.
"I think I'll join you."

Before Kitty and Dog could reply, Pig squished between them. Things were *extra* cozy.

Kitty, Dog, and Pig wobbled near the coop.

"No need to shout," said Rooster as he perched atop Pig's head. Luckily, there was exactly enough space for a medium-sized rooster.

"*Coat-a-doodle-doo!*" said you-know-who.

Kitty, Dog, Pig, and Rooster tottered toward the pasture.

It was a tighty-whitie fit.

Kitty, Dog, Pig, Rooster, and Cow practically rolled past the pond.

Kitty, Dog, Pig, Rooster, Cow, and Bird tumbled into the air and all around.

What a way to end the day.

Kitty, Dog, Pig, Rooster, Cow, and Bird said their goodbyes.

"Ah . . ." said Kitty.

AUTHOR'S NOTE

Years ago, when I was a library media specialist, I loved to share Jan Brett's *The Mitten* with my students. Brett's book is based on an old Ukrainian folktale. Other versions of this story exist, such as the one by Alvin Tresselt, but the original author is unknown.

The Underpants offers some similarities to *The Mitten* as well as some differences. These variations include an extra dose of silliness, a new cast of characters, and a setting that is very much like that of my childhood home. I also exchanged a perfectly nice mitten for a pair of underpants.

My characters, however, would most certainly tell you, "It's a coat!"

For teachers everywhere — especially Miss Rome, Mrs. Werner,
Mrs. Zellmer, Mrs. Piatt, and Mrs. Colwell. — TS

Text copyright © 2022 by Tammi Sauer
Illustrations copyright © 2022 by Joren Cull

Library of Congress Cataloging-in-Publication Data available

ISBN 978-1-338-74027-1

10 9 8 7 6 5 4 3 2 1   22 23 24 25 26

Printed in China   62
First edition, October 2022

Book design by Charles Kreloff

The type was set in Bitstream Cooper Medium.
The artwork was drawn by hand and then colored in Adobe Photoshop.